Sister, Sister

written and illustrated by
Anne Sibley O'Brien

Bebop Book.
An imprint of LEE & LOW BOOKS Inc.

D1376873

I like to sing songs.

My sister likes to listen to music.

I like to play make believe.

My sister likes to study her rocks.

I like to make noise when I play.

My sister likes to be quiet.

I like to make a mess in our room.

My sister likes to keep things neat.

I like to listen to stories.

My sister likes to read stories.

I love my sister.